To Christopher Wheeldon and the dancers of the New York City Ballet—J. L.

To Yelena, Max, and Archie—B. K.

SIMON & SCHUSTER
BOOKS FOR YOUNG READERS
An imprint of Simon & Schuster Children's Publishing Division • 1230 Avenue of the Americas, New York, New York 10020 • Text copyright © 2004 by John Lithgow • Illustrations copyright © 2004 by Boris Kulikov • All rights reserved, including the right of reproduction in whole or in part in any form. • Photograph on pages 36–37 © Paul Kolnik • SIMON & SCHUSTER BOOKS FOR YOUNG READERS is a trademark of Simon & Schuster, Inc. • Book design by Dan Potash • The text for this book is set in Andromeda. • The illustrations for this book are rendered in watercolor and gouache. • Manufactured in China 1 2 3 4 5 6 7 8 9 10 • Library of Congress Cataloging-in-Publication Data • Lithgow, John, 1945– • Carnival of the animals / by John Lithgow; illustrated by Boris Kulikov.— 1st ed. p. cm. Summary: A mischievous boy slips away from his teacher during a field trip to a natural history museum and, after the museum closes, sees all of the people he knows transformed into animals. • ISBN 0-689-86721-2 [1. Animals—Fiction. 2. Museums—Fiction. 3. Imagination—Fiction. 4. Field trips—Fiction. 5. Stories in rhyme] I. Kulikov, Boris, ill. II. Title. PZ83.L6375 Car 2004 • [E]—dc21 2003009595

first edition

Carnival
of the
Animals

by John Lithgow

illustrated by Boris Kulikov

Simon & Schuster Books for Young Readers

NEW YORK   LONDON   TORONTO   SYDNEY

Oliver Pendleton Percy the Third
Was a mischievous imp of a lad.
The tricks that he played on Professor McByrd
Nearly drove the old schoolmaster mad.

One day, with his schoolmates, he climbed up the stairs
To the Natural History Museum,
Where, catching Professor McByrd unawares,
He ran past a sign that said UNDER REPAIRS,
Then hid amidst antelopes, beavers, and bears,
Where none of the others could see 'im.

And since nobody knew where the rascal had crept,
Closing time passed and young Oliver slept.

In the room where the slumbering schoolboy was hidden,
Caressed by the moon's ghostly beams,
The stately stuffed animals awakened, unbidden,
Inhabiting Oliver's dreams.

The buffalo bellowed, the falcon took flight,
The tail of the peacock unfurled.
But among them emerged an astonishing sight:
Pale apparitions invading the night.
In place of the animals, into the light
Stepped the people from Oliver's world.

For example, the students who went to his school
Were hyenas, determined to break every rule.
And in shabby brown tweeds with an old yellow tie on,
Professor McByrd was turned into a lion!

Oliver's watch said eleven o'clock.

The shadows continued to thicken.

From the darkness came strutting a fluttering flock,

The parents of all of the kids on his block.

Each father was now a cantankerous cock

And each mother a fussbudget chicken.

Rodents raced in, like a pack of wet cats,
All snapping and nipping and nibbling.
The ferrets and badgers and weasels and rats
Were sticky-faced toddlers and snotty-nosed brats,
A species that always drove Oliver bats:
The Greater New York younger sibling.

Near Oliver's house lived a dotty old pair,
Two twins, Aspidistra and Myrtle.
In the park every Sunday they'd sit and they'd stare,
Recalling their years with the Folies Bergère.
Then they'd kick their identical heels in the air
At the pace of a graceful old turtle.

Displaying more strength than a strapping young man can,
Two elderly tortoises, dancing the cancan.

Mabel Buntz, the school nurse, lumbered into the hall,
The scourge of each virus and germ.
Though Nurse Buntz was decidedly wider than tall,
Her size didn't hamper her movements at all
When she daintily waltzed at the Elephant Ball,
A flirtatious and pert pachyderm.

And there, with an air of tremulous grace,
Stood a fretful and frail kangaroo.
Oliver studied her wallflower face,
Her hand-me-down dress with her grandmother's lace.
Why on earth was she here, in this unlikely place,
His librarian, Miss Marian Prue?

But Miss Prue in her dreams was not nearly so shy,
For her dreams fulfilled all of her wishes.
Oliver spied, in the gleam of her eye,
Cinema sirens from ages gone by.
They'd invite her to join them, and off they would fly,
Like diaphanous tropical fishes.

She floated among them all, gloating with pleasure,
A mermaid protecting a vast sunken treasure.

All the freckly schoolgirls in Oliver's class
Left him gasping, and grasping for words.
When they squealed in the hall or they sprawled on the grass,
His face was aflame as he'd timidly pass.
But tonight, full of flighty excitement and sass,
They were flocks of exotic young birds.

Oliver smiled, relaxed and unwary,
Lit up by the gleam of his dream aviary.

Jackasses dashed through the gallery door;
They shook every window and beam.
Though Oliver shrunk from their deafening roar,
He distinctly remembered he'd seen them before,
Storming across the gymnasium floor,
The boys on the wrestling team.

In front of the girls, they were bluff and hard-bitten,
But clearly the asses were secretly smitten.

On Saturday mornings from ten until noon
Poor Oliver practiced his scales.
His teacher, the maestro Herr Doktor von Loon,
Whose lessons included no hint of a tune,
Resembled a manic-depressive baboon
Whose shrieks could be heard in North Wales.

A cuckoo sits weeping, bereft in her nest.
Her chick has been missing since noon.
She pictures him hungry, a cold in his chest,
Insufficiently fed, insufficiently dressed.
She fears that her poor heart will burst in her breast
If some news of him doesn't come soon.

Is the cuckoo a cuckoo? Or perhaps something other?
The fact is, the cuckoo is Oliver's mother.

Once, Oliver's class went to see a ballet
And arrived like a herd of young cattle.
The dusty production they put on display
Was a hundred and fifty years old, if a day,
A gargantuan, pink brontosaurus at play.
You could practically hear the bones rattle.

But at every ballet, in her own private box,
Sat Oliver's great-aunt Cecile,
Wearing tea-rose perfume and a stole of red fox.
Her memories of girlhood turned back all the clocks
To the night when the audience lined up for blocks
To see her Odette and Odile.

With her ivory neck and her downy chiffon,
Not a woman at all, but an elegant swan.

A silvery light filtered into the room.
The day was about to begin.
The displays were as silent and still as a tomb,
When a kindly night watchman strolled in.

It was he who discovered the sleeping young lad
And sent Oliver home, good as new.
When the boy was returned to his mother and dad,
His emotions were split between happy and sad.
But oh! what a fabulous night he had had,
When his world was turned into a zoo!

The next midnight each beast reawakened with glee,
For Oliver Percy had set them all free.

New York City Ballet choreographer Christopher Wheeldon set out to create a new ballet based on Camille Saint-Saëns's orchestral suite *Carnival of the Animals*. He asked children's book author John Lithgow to help him devise a premise to turn the suite into a story for children and to write a rhyming narration. The ballet opened to great acclaim on May 14, 2003, with Mr. Lithgow speaking the narration and performing the role of Mabel Buntz, the school nurse. The entire New York City Ballet cast is pictured here.

The ballet's narration provided the text for this book.